W9-BJT-936

A Beginning-to-Read Book

I Need You, Dear Dragon

by Margaret Hillert
Illustrated by David Helton

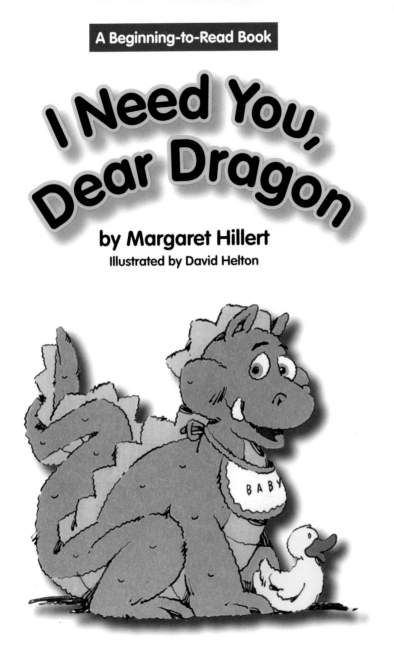

NORWOOD HOUSE PRESS

DEAR CAREGIVER,

The *Beginning-to-Read* series is a carefully written collection of classic readers you may remember from your own childhood. Each book features text comprised of common sight words to provide your child ample practice reading the words that appear most frequently in written text. The many additional details in the pictures enhance the story and offer the opportunity for you to help your child expand oral language and develop comprehension.

Begin by reading the story to your child, followed by letting him or her read familiar words and soon your child will be able to read the story independently. At each step of the way, be sure to praise your reader's efforts to build his or her confidence as an independent reader. Discuss the pictures and encourage your child to make connections between the story and his or her own life. At the end of the story, you will find reading activities and a word list that will help your child practice and strengthen beginning reading skills.

Above all, the most important part of the reading experience is to have fun and enjoy it!

Shannon Cannon

Shannon Cannon,
Literacy Consultant

Norwood House Press • P.O. Box 316598 • Chicago, Illinois 60631
For more information about Norwood House Press please visit our website at
www.norwoodhousepress.com or call 866-565-2900.

LIBRARY OF CONGRESS CATALOGING-IN-PUBLICATION DATA

Hillert, Margaret.
  I need you, dear dragon / by Margaret Hillert ; illustrated by David
Helton. — Rev. and expanded library ed.
     p. cm. — (Beginning to read series. Dear dragon)
  Summary: Dear dragon feels somewhat rejected when his master's new baby
sister comes home from the hospital, but love and reassurance put things
right. Includes reading activities.
  ISBN-13: 978-1-59953-039-0 (library binding : alk. paper)
  ISBN-10: 1-59953-039-2 (library binding : alk. paper)
  [1. Babies—Fiction. 2. Dragons—Fiction.] I. Helton, David, ill. II.
Title. III. Series: Hillert, Margaret. Beginning to read series. Dear dragon.
  PZ7.H558Iam 2007
  [E]—dc22   2006007089

Beginning-to-Read series (c) 2007 by Margaret Hillert.
Library edition published by permission of Pearson Education, Inc. in
arrangement with Norwood House Press, Inc. All rights reserved.
This book was originally published by Follett Publishing Company in 1985.
Manufactured in the United States of America in North Mankato, Minnesota - 154R-022010

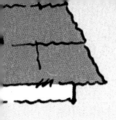

Here comes the car.
Oh, here comes the car.
I see Mother.
Mother is home.

Mother, Mother.
Now you are home.
That is good.

4

5

Is that the baby?
I want to see it.
Oh, I want to see it!

Oh, my. Oh, my.
A little, little baby.

What a pretty baby!
What a pretty baby it is.
Look, look.

In here.
In here.
This is where we go.

This is something for
the baby —

and this —

and this.

Father, Father.
Can I have the baby?
I want the baby.

My, what a pretty one.
So little, little.
I like you, little baby.

Here, Mother.
This is a good little baby.
I like her.

Oh, there you are.
You did not come in.
We want you to come in.

See.
Here is something that
looks like you.
It is for the baby.

19

The baby will like it.
Yes, yes.
The baby will like it.

Come here. Come here.
You can do something here.
Come on.
Oh, come on.

See now.
Look what you can do.
This is a good thing for
you to do.

Look at that.
The baby likes you.
And I like you, too.
I do. I do.

The baby is little.
Too little to play with me now.
But you and I can play.

We can play and have fun.
Come on with me.
Come on and play.
Run, run, run.

Here you are with me.
And here I am with you.
I need you.
I need you, dear dragon.

READING REINFORCEMENT

The following activities support the findings of the National Reading Panel that determined the most effective components for reading instruction are: Phonemic Awareness, Phonics, Vocabulary, Fluency, and Text Comprehension.

Phonemic Awareness: The /y/ sound

Oral Blending: Say the beginning and ending sounds of the following words and ask your child to listen to the sounds and say the whole word:

/y/ + ou = you   /y/ + es = yes   /y/ + ear = year
/y/ + am = yam   /y/ + arn = yarn   /y/ + uck = yuck
/y/ + ard = yard   /y/ + ellow = yellow

Phonics: The letter Yy

1. Demonstrate how to form the letters **Y** and **y** for your child.
2. Have your child practice writing **Y** and **y** at least three times each.
3. Ask your child to point to the words in the book that have the letter **y** in them.
4. Write down the following words and ask your child to circle the letter **y** in each word:

yes	you	baby	my	funny
money	key	young	cycle	pretty
your	silly	cry	maybe	yard

Vocabulary: Adjectives

1. Explain to your child that words that describe something are called adjectives.

2. Say the following nouns and ask your child to name an adjective that might be used to describe it (possible answers in parentheses):

car (fast)	flower (pretty)	candy (sweet)
snake (slimy)	clown (funny)	sun (bright)
cotton (soft)	mansion (big)	ice (cold)

3. Ask your child to name the adjectives that might be used to describe babies. (Possible answers: pretty, tiny, cute, cuddly, sweet, soft, wiggly, little, chubby, noisy, etc.)

4. Write the words on separate pieces of paper.

5. Mix the words up and read each word aloud to your child. Encourage your child to explain how the adjective describes babies.

6. Mix the words up again and randomly say each word to your child. Ask your child to point to the correct word.

Fluency: Shared Reading

1. Reread the story to your child at least two more times while your child tracks the print by running a finger under the words as they are read. Ask your child to read the words he or she knows with you.

2. Reread the story taking turns, alternating readers between sentences or pages.

Text Comprehension: Discussion Time

1. Ask your child to retell the sequence of events in the story.

2. To check comprehension, ask your child the following questions:

   • Where do you think the boy's mother and father were?

   • What are the things the family has for the baby on pages 11-13?

   • How does the boy feel about having a new baby in the family? How do you know?

   • How does Dear Dragon help the baby?

   • Do you think you would make a good big brother or sister? Why?

WORD LIST

I Need You, Dear Dragon **uses the 60 words listed below.**
This list can be used to practice reading the words that appear in the text. You
may wish to write the words on index cards and use them to help your child
build automatic word recognition. Regular practice with these words will
enhance your child's fluency in reading connected text.

a	Father	like	play	want
am	for	little	pretty	we
and	fun	look		what
are			run	where
at	go	me		will
	good	Mother	see	with
baby		my	so	
but	have		something	yes
	her	need		you
can	here	not	that	
car	home	now	the	
come			there	
	I	oh	thing	
dear	in	on	this	
did	is	one	to	
do	it		too	
dragon				

ABOUT THE AUTHOR Margaret Hillert has written over 80 books for
children who are just learning to read. Her books
have been translated into many different languages and over a million children
throughout the world have read her books. She first started writing poetry as
a child and has continued to write for children and adults throughout her life. A
first grade teacher for 34 years, Margaret is now retired from teaching and lives in
Michigan where she likes to write, take walks in the morning, and care for her three cats.

Photograph by Glenna Washburn

ABOUT THE ADVISER Shannon Cannon contributed the activities pages that appear in
this book. Shannon serves as a literacy consultant and provides
staff development to help improve reading instruction. She is a frequent presenter at educational
conferences and workshops. Prior to this she worked as an elementary school teacher and as
president of a curriculum publishing company.